DARTH MAUL'S MISSION

BY ACE LANDERS   ILLUSTRATED BY DAVID WHITE

ISBN 978-0-545-30441-2

LEGO, THE LEGO LOGO, THE BRICK AND KNOB CONFIGURATIONS AND THE MINIFIGURE ARE TRADEMARKS OF THE LEGO GROUP. © 2011 THE LEGO GROUP. PRODUCED BY SCHOLASTIC INC. UNDER LICENSE FROM THE LEGO GROUP.

PUBLISHED BY SCHOLASTIC INC. SCHOLASTIC AND ASSOCIATED LOGOS ARE TRADEMARKS AND/OR REGISTERED TRADEMARKS OF SCHOLASTIC INC.

12 11 10 9 8 7   12 13 14 15/0

PRINTED IN THE U.S.A.   40

FIRST PRINTING, AUGUST 2011

SCHOLASTIC INC.

NEW YORK   TORONTO   LONDON   AUCKLAND   SYDNEY   MEXICO CITY   NEW DELHI   HONG KONG

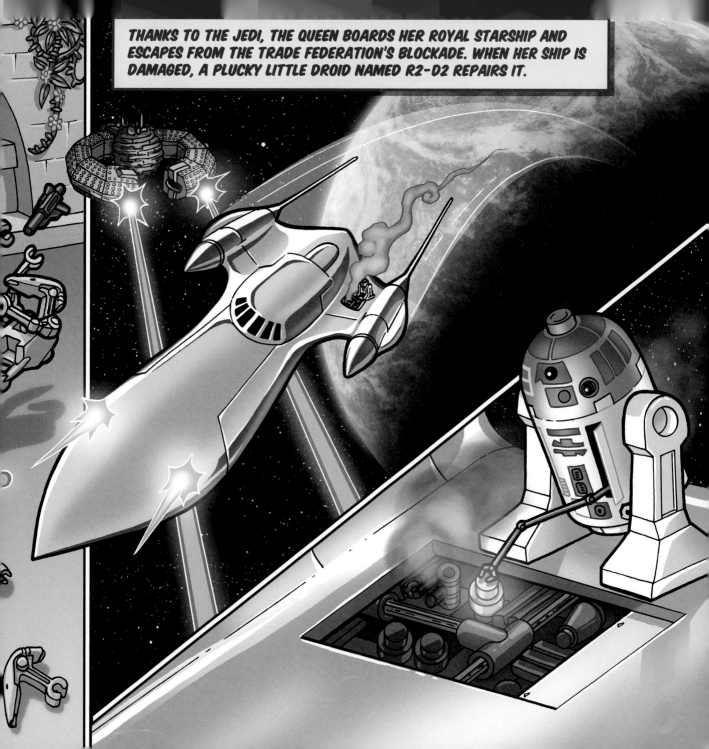

DARTH MAUL AND QUI-GON CLASH, DODGE, AND SLASH AT EACH OTHER. THE SOUNDS OF STRIKING LIGHTSABERS SLICE THROUGH THE DESERT AIR.

THE QUEEN FLIES BACK TO NABOO TO FIGHT THE TRADE FEDERATION ARMY, BUT DARTH MAUL IS WAITING FOR HER LOYAL JEDI KNIGHTS.

AND FINALLY THE HEROES CAN PARTY.